BAIL LIFE VOLUME 2
PCP

Michael Doc Reaves

Copyright © 2019 Michael Doc Reaves
ISBN:
ISBN-978-0-578-21633-1

Contents

ACKNOWLEDGMENTS

THANKS TO DEVA , LATINA, JUNE, AND CARTER FOR
ALLOWING ME TO USE THEIR NAMES AS CHARACTERS IN
THIS FICTIONAL STORY.

Thanks to Charita, Amari and Maiya for help with editing.

Special Thanks to Maiya for using her special creative talents during editing.

Chapter 1

{Music playing}
I'm your Bondsman that's
who I am and I'm
ready to bail whoever
I can call me early
Morning or late afternoon.

Poochie: Hey baby, are you still looking for Alex?

Me: Oh yeah, have you heard anything?

Poochie: I hear he is running with a gang now his street name is Ajax. He's the brains if you can believe that. His guys are getting into carjacking and robberies.

Me: Do you know where he sleeps at around here?

Poochie: No, but they have a pipeline of drugs going to Johnson City, Tennessee. He must be making some money. He's driving around in a new Silver Mustang.
Me: Thanks, Poochie. You doing ok?

Poochie: I could use a few dollars if you got it.

Me: I'll meet you at Pot Luck quickie mart on Rauhut in about fifteen minutes.

Poochie: Thanks baby.

Most people call me Doc, I'm a Bail bondsman and Real Estate Agent in North Carolina. I live a busy life with a wife and three children, two of which have gone on to their careers. One in California, one in Missouri, and the last one making her way through Middle school. My wife spends her days either caring for her aging parents or substitute teaching.

Bail bonding is the process of getting people out of jail when they get arrested and then, putting them back if they don't go to court. I have a bail runner that helps me do that named Deva. A lot of people call him "Big Deva," with good reason, Deva is around 6'6" and about 340 lbs. He has a teddy bear disposition, as long as you don't offend him. We have an office in Graham North Carolina across the street from the jail and courthouse. My business requires me to be on the phone a lot.

The last time Deva and I were together, I received a phone call about a guy that hadn't gone to court named Alex Chandler, now called Ajax. He was a small-time drug dealer that wasn't a violent person. In fact, a lot of people liked him, which always makes it tougher to find a person. The phone call was from one of my informants named Poochie. She was a frequent client of mine once in her life. Poochie has turned her life into a different direction, but as she says, "she is a work in progress." When Poochie calls, she usually has useful information for me.

I had been to Johnson City before to pick up a bail bond skip named Tommy Coble. He was one of the easiest pickups Deva, and I ever had.

I remember the trip. We had driven the 3 hours to Johnson City before we realized we didn't even take Tommy's picture to show the detective what he looked like. Without a picture, finding Tommy could be a problem. Thankfully, Tommy had distinct features. A lazy right eye, short (about 5'5") and a 150 lbs. He had a way of talking that made him easy to describe. His speech was slow and very country. Detective Gasparello was the Narcotics agent we made contact with at the police department in Johnson City. Detective Gasparello was extremely happy to see us when we showed up. We presented our credentials and stated why we were there. Johnson City was having a problem with the influx of people from Burlington coming there selling drugs. The kids in Burlington could get drugs cheaper than they could in Johnson City. Burlington is right off of Highway 40 which is the main line for drugs moving across the U.S. The Burlington low-level dealers could go there and instantly become big-time dealers. Gasparello knew about the problem and the Burlington guys being there and had dealt with a lot of trouble but could not find a way to get rid of them. Finding out we were there to take one out of town was music to his ears.

The Detective knew that a guy fitting Tommy's description, liked to come out at night and cruise with his girlfriend. She was a local girl they knew very well. He was so happy; he called a local hotel to get me and Deva a room at a discounted rate. I gave Gasparello my phone number and me and Deva went to the hotel and checked in.

Johnson City is a small town, about the size of Burlington, in a mountainous area with beautiful views. It was a good, 3-hour drive from Burlington, but Deva and I had come up from a bail bond class that day in Charlotte, which was 3 hours away from Johnson City in the opposite direction. We were pretty tired and needed to eat and get some sleep before we picked Tommy up for the ride back to the jail in Graham. Graham is the county seat for Alamance County, so they housed all the people locked up in the County. When we got to the hotel, we talked to some people that worked there. It turned out that the people at the hotel were also familiar with the Burlington group of troublemakers. They were trying to figure out how to keep them out of their hotel legally.

After we checked in, Deva and I stopped at a Chinese buffet with all of the signature foods of an Asian restaurant. I don't think they had prepared for a man of Deva's appetite that evening. I looked at Deva's first plate, it would have fed a small family. I saw the cook and the hostess speaking in Mandarin and pointing at some empty pans and rushing back and forth to the kitchen. We filled up before going back to the hotel to get some sleep. I set my phone alarm to 10:00 pm, but at 9:30pm we were awakened by my song playing. My cellphone ringtone and ringback tone is *I'm your Bondsman*, an original song written by one of my old clients. I keep it as a reminder for family and friends to do everything they can to get their loved ones out of jail. I answered the call, and Detective Gasparello was on the phone telling me that he thinks he's got Tommy stopped, but he is giving him a different name. He needed me and Deva to get over to Main Street and identify him as soon as possible.

Everyone uses a nickname these days, so it's hard to know who's who. Deva and I loaded up everything and headed his way. When we pulled up, we saw two police cars sitting with a

car pulled over. I got out of the car walked over and saw Tommy looking down at the floorboards shaking his head. When he saw me get out of the car, he knew it was over. I thanked the officers and pulled out my handcuffs with the short chain and ankle bracelets. The short chain made for a much nicer ride, than having his hands handcuffed behind his back. That way he could keep them in front while hooked up to his feet and sit more comfortably. I hooked Tommy up, and Deva patted him down for weapons and placed him in the front seat of the car beside me. Once we hooked his seat belt tight, Tommy's girlfriend started crying, saying she would come and get him back out. All I could think of was "Love would find a way." If getting Ajax is anything like getting Tommy Coble, I'm thinking Ajax being in Johnson City shouldn't be a big problem for us.
{Ringing}

Gasparello: Hello?

Me: Detective Gasparello this is Doc Reaves from Burlington; North Carolina I came up there about a year ago and picked up Tommy Coble.

Gasparello: Oh yes. How are you doing?

Me: I'm great. We have another problem over there and was wondering if you'd heard anything about him.

Gasparello: What's the name? If he's from Burlington, I'm sure we've had some contact with him.

Me: Alex Chandler. His street name is Ajax and he's into the drug game.

Gasparello: Oh yea, I know him well. We are doing an investigation on his crew about a murder in the City of Bristol. We had a young girl from a well to do family get killed near an apartment complex his gang hangs out at. When are you coming up to get him?

Me: It will probably be this Saturday.

Gasparello: No problem. I know where his boys live and hang out. We have an apartment across the parking lot from his crew, that we use to get information on them. The landlord lets us use the place to keep some of the trouble out of the area. I'll let you guys use it

when you come up. He's going to be there for sure.
Me: You guys are incredible. I appreciate it. I'll call you when we get there.

(Music playing)
They locked me up with
no place to go, they took
my clothes and stole
my doe. I'm in a cell on
A pay phone, call my
bondsman and get me
 home. (Get me home)

Deva has a ringback tone by the same client called "Get Me Home" that has a country sound to it.

Deva: What's up? (Deva always uses his caller i.d. to jump right into the conversation).

Me: I want to go to Johnson City to pick up Ajax on Saturday.

Deva: Sounds good to me. What time you want to head up there? I'm planning on being up late watching wrestling.

Me: I want to leave around 6:00 am and get an early start.

Deva: Come on through. I'll be ready. (Click… Deva doesn't waste time with goodbyes either).

Chapter 2

It was Monday. Unofficially, my golf day. I always like to go by the office and get a few things done before, I get missing on the golf course. The office was open when I got there. Latina was doing some filing and straightening around the office. Latina is the office receptionist, information gatherer, and chief enforcer of time management. She runs the office a lot more efficiently than I ever could. I met Latina about six years earlier at the jail. She was taking charges out on her abusive husband at the time. They later divorced. She came by looking for a job and has been here ever since. Latina is half Puerto Rican, half Black and 100% quick witted.

Latina: Hey, what's going on? We got some more forfeitures coming from the courthouse. Mrs. Sylvia called and said we had four yesterday. One of them was J Rock, we have been getting him out for years. He's got a problem picking up stuff that doesn't belong to him and not giving it back.

Me: Wow, that's a lot for one day. I hope some of them just forgot they had court. (Not likely).

Latina: I'll look them up and make a few calls to see what the deal is with them. What time is tee time today?

Me: 11:20.

Latina: Don't let them take your money today. June called earlier looking for you. He said he was going to take care of you today if you show up. I asked him to take it easy on you. I told him we hadn't gotten paid yet. (She said with a smirk)
June is about 70 years old and in great shape for a guy his age. We've been beating each

other for years on the golf course along with about 15 other guys on Mondays and Fridays. Right then a guy entered the office with a sign saying "Homeless" on a piece of cardboard. He stood there looking around for about 8 seconds. He was about 5'6", dark complexion, slim, wearing blue jeans and a Carolina Blue shirt that said UNC. He seemed to be about thirty-five years old, the cardboard sign neatly folded under his arm. So, I asked:

Me: Can I help you?

Homeless guy: Do you guys take a retainer for bail bonds?

Me: What do you mean? where are you from? Do you have a warrant or something?

Homeless guy: I'm from Hillsborough. (A town about fifteen miles away) No. I don't have any warrants yet, but suppose I get stopped driving with no license? How much would it cost to make a bond like that?

Me: What kind of car do you have?

Homeless guy: I don't have one. I'm going to get one before the day is over though. (with a shifty look in his eye)

Me: Really?

Homeless guy: I've got to go. I'm tired. It's been a long day. (walks out).

Me: (Turning to Latina) Did you lock your doors on your car?

Latina: I hope so.

Later that day on hole number 18 at Indian Valley golf course. I found myself staring down the putt, I needed to keep, June from winning a bet. The day goes a lot better when I beat him but preventing him from winning works just as good. It was a six-footer with a little left to right break. I could feel the intense stare on the ball coming from June. He was trying as hard as he could to mind pull the ball out of the hole and get away with a win. I pulled back the putter and just as I stroke the putt, my phone starts vibrating in my pocket and the putt missed to the right. June let out a deep breath saying "Whew, that was close! Great putt!" and a big grin spread all across his face.

*I'm your Bondsman that's
who I am and I'm
ready to bail whoever
I can call me early
Morning or late afternoon.*

Me: Reaves.

Kat: Doc, Man. These cops out here keep harassing me. Every time I pull out the driveway I get pulled over. I'm tired of it, what can I do?

Me: Why are they stopping you, they got to have a reason?

Kat: Man, just anything. They just pulled me and had me spread eagle in the middle of the street. People riding by looking. You know they act like a black man can't drive a Lexus with rims on it. Next thing I know, here comes that dog. We should be on a first name bases as much as they call him for me. He went around the car three times before one of the cops kicked my side door, and he barked. They're trying to tell me that was a signal that there were drugs in there. I started to cuss them out, but I knew it wasn't anything in there so, I told them my lawyer was going to have a field day. Man, they had that dog all up in my ride.

Me: Yeah, I would call my attorney on that one. Did they find anything?

Kat: Nah, I stopped selling when I got out last time. Man the 12's (police) doing some funky stuff out here in these streets right now. I'm going to call my attorney right now.

Me: He might get you to get a restraining order so they can't stop you anymore.

Kat: Thanks, bro.

After I finished listening to June talk junk, about me missing that putt and settling up, I decide to stop by the courts on the way home. I love to go by the basketball courts to see who's playing and talk with the guys. Everybody's got some story going on. When I pull up, I can see some of the overweight guys that should have given up the game about ten years ago, shooting around. Mostly, they go out there to hack and vent some work frustrations. It's tough when you can't keep up with the young boys and have to hold on to play defense without being embarrassed. Putt was out there today. He is another one of my sources of information on the street. Putt is thirty-two years old and well respected, an O.G. He earned his respect by shooting a guy trying to crawl out of his window when he came home from work early. We very rarely speak in public so, he kept shooting on the other end of the court, and I talked to the rest of the guys about Ajax. Everyone on the court knew who I was or had heard of me from bail bonding or basketball. I used to play a lot and had a playground legend's reputation. Most guys knew about the gang Ajax was in and were reluctant to say anything. Which doesn't surprise me. I usually expect that if someone wants to talk, they will call me later and see what's in it for them. One guy was out there selling hot dogs and beers. Another guy was trying to get some heckling going.

P Rick: Why didn't you get me out of jail when I called you two months ago?

Me: What's your name?

P Rick: P Rick. My government name is Patrick Pulliam you act like you don't do credit.

Me: I do credit if you got some way of paying and someone to sign for you.

P Rick: Man, I can get the money. Next time I call you, you need to come and get me out of jail! (shaking his head)

Me: Who got you out?

P Rick: The court gave me time served after I ate that nasty food for a month. They should have given me an iron stomach certificate. (chuckling) That food was unseasoned, cold, or hard to get your teeth through.

The court will eventually let you out if they feel you have served enough time for your crime and couldn't make bail.

P Rick: Hey, why are the cops riding so hard? I saw them earlier with some guy out in the middle of the street looking like he was doing yoga or something. I got some video of it for my blog.

*I'm your Bondsman that's
who I am and I'm
ready to bail whoever
I can call me early
Morning or late afternoon.*

Me: Hey.

Charita: I'm going to a meeting tonight about the school board changing school zones. I probably won't be in before 9 pm. What time are you coming home?

Me: I'm heading that way soon. What did you cook?

Charita: Swedish Meatballs, mashed potatoes, and green peas.

Me: That sounds good. Where's Amari?

Charita: I'm going to pick her up on my way to the meeting. She had choir practice today at the church.

Me: Ok. I'll see you when you get home.

Charita: Bye, Big Poppy. {chuckling}

My wife Charita is one in a million, especially in today's times. She still cooks, and I have a magic sock draw that keeps filling up with clean socks automatically. She's nice looking, with a great sense of humor.

I'm your Bondsman that's
who I am and I'm
ready to bail whoever
I can call me early

Morning or late afternoon.

You have a phone call from Rod Roader an Inmate at the Alamance County detention center push one to accept. Beep.
Me: Reaves. What can I help you with?

Inmate Rod: Can you come down and get me out? I got pulled over for failing to stop at a stop sign. They said the car smelled like weed. My car doesn't smell like weed. I keep air fresheners in it all the time!

Me: Where are you from? You sound like you're from up north, and how much is your bond?

Rod: I'm from New Jersey but, I go to Elon. I'm taking criminal justice, this is going to mess me up. I got a five-thousand-dollar bond. My friends have the money downstairs. It's ten percent, right?

Me: Have you called your parents?

Rod: My Dad's a lawyer in New Jersey. I called him when I got pulled. I thought it was something simple, but when the officer started talking about searching the car, my dad said, "Don't let him search without a warrant." That's when they called for the dog. That thing went crazy in my car! I had a quarter pound of weed in the car. They took that and brought me down here.

Me: Ok, get your Dad to call me. I'll call Deva to come down and post the bond for you to get out.

Rod: Thanks

They locked me up with
no place to go, they took
my clothes and stole
my doe. I'm in a cell on
A pay phone, call my
bondsman and get me
 home. (Get me home)

Deva: Sup

Me: Hey Deva can you get a "Rod Roader" out of the Alamance County Jail?

Deva: Doc, right now I'm up in Greensboro at a repair shop. My Escalade doesn't want to start sometimes. I hope it's not going to take too long.

Me: It's no problem Deva. I'll take care of it.

Deva: I'll call you when I get back. This thing is starting to be a pain. Every time I go about twenty miles away from home, it wants to breakdown.

I don't get to the jail all that often because Deva takes care of most of the bonds. The jail was swarming with officers when I went into the lobby. The jail is solid concrete with tile floors and tall ceilings. The Sheriff came walking in like a man on a mission.

Sheriff: Hey Doc. How's your business going?

Me: Not bad Sheriff.

Sheriff: Well, it's about to get a whole lot better. I got "all hands-on deck," and I'm shutting down all drug operations in this county. We've got some scum bags selling Phencyclidine. It's called PCP on the street. I'm going after every drug dealer I can find, and we are going to send a message. Everything we take off the streets is going to the lab until we find out where it's coming from and when we find them.........We are going to put them away for a long time. There are some reports of kids going crazy and jumping off houses. You know I can't stand drugs, but now it's gotten personal.

There was a lot of people around the jail that day. Some asking questions and others there to get people out of jail. One couple was there to get married. What a backdrop for your forever after.

Sheriff: Who are you here to get out Doc?

Me: I'm here for the Elon kid that got picked up on the weed charge.

Sheriff: Oh him. He was smoking weed when he got pulled by my deputy. My officer told me when he asked him to roll down the window, he should have been wearing a gas mask. He almost got a contact himself. The kid was on the phone with his Dad, telling him he didn't know why he stopped him. He was only driving about fifteen miles per hour and slowly rolled through the stop sign, almost hitting another car. Then the father told him not to let the officers search the car, so he called for Jammer our Canine. As soon as he got on scene, the dog started trying to jump out of the car. He was signaling from inside the patrol car. They didn't even take him out of the car! You better keep your phone on because we've got a lot more coming and we need to make some room in the jail.

Me: You know I will Sheriff. Be safe.

Sheriff: Same to you Doc.

The Elon kids usually come from well to do families and looking at Rod when he came out, he fit the profile. Rod walked out of jail wearing a Fraternity shirt, golf shorts, and was immediately hailed by his crew as, the new "God Father" of Elon.

Me: Is that skunk I smell?

College roommate: That's some of that high-grade Hydro weed you smell. (While he was paying for the bail)

Me: I've got to fill out this information and send your dad an indemnity agreement Rod. I'm your bail bondsman, Doc Reaves.

Rod: Man, I'm telling you, I shouldn't be here. This guy was looking to arrest someone to make some quota or something. I still don't know why they stopped me.

 After filling out all the necessary paperwork, I went back to the office to send Rod's dad the indemnity agreement. Soon after, I was walking in the house to relax in my recliner and channel surf. I love watching The First 48 murder investigative show. Bail Bonding is a 24-hour service with calls all through the night, so it did not take long for me to start dozing off. When I woke up I saw a body on the screen, laid back, toes up, with a sheet over him. One of the bodies being investigated for evidence on the "First 48".

Chapter 3

I'm your Bondsman that's
who I am and I'm
ready to bail whoever
I can call me early
Morning or late afternoon.

Me: Hello.

Poochie: Hey Doc. It's Poochie. I'm at this house, and somebody said you were looking for Shabazz.

Me: Oh yeah, he just skipped this week.

Poochie: He's over here at 527 Short St. right now running that mouth. I'm outside now, but I'll hang around for a while if you want and see where he goes.

Me: I'm on my way.
They locked me up with
no place to go, they took
my clothes and stole
my doe. I'm in a cell on
A pay phone, call my
bondsman and get me
 home. (Get me home)

Deva: Yeah?

Me: Are you close?

Deva: Yep. I'm back in town. What's up?

Me: Shabazz is on 527 Short St.

Deva: I'm on my way.

Me: Meet me at Robinson Park down the street from the house.

Deva: Got it.

Shabazz has a long record of conning people out of money. He's a great talker for people that will listen.
His bond was 5000.00 dollars when we bailed him out for conning some old people. He decided not to show up for court after he found out the people he defrauded was related to a

local judge. Shabazz just missed court last week, so I hadn't offered a reward for him yet. A quick pick up would be great.

Deva came dressed in a nice yellow dress shirt and blue dress pants. Deva was always a good dresser, but I'm sure he had other plans for the outfit. I just looked him up and down with a question in my eye.

Deva: Jah (Deva's son), had a school banquet.

Me: You look good. How was it?

Deva: He won most improved for the horn.

Me: The best students come from the band, you should be proud.

Deva: His mom put him in it.

Deva, like most dads wants his son to follow in his footsteps. Deva was an All-State basketball player in high school and played in college.

Deva slid into the passenger seat of my Toyota Avalon and we started down toward Short Street. Looking at the different houses in the neighborhood, you could see small two- and three-bedroom ranch style homes with a few street lights. It is an older community and some of the homes were around 50-60 years

old. Pulling up one block over from the house, we get out and start walking up. Deva heads toward the back door while I keep going toward the front porch. It's almost as long as the house. I slipped up to one of the front porch windows and peek into what looks like the living room. Shabazz is sitting there laughing at the TV with a beer in front of him. Seeing that he's in there, I move to the front door, knocking lightly as though I was invited.
Homeowner: (from inside the door) Who is it?

Me: Doc Reaves, Bail Bondsman.

Homeowner: Just a minute....... I'll be right there.

There is no getting out once we are in position, but to make sure, I peek into the window again; and Shabazz is gone. I walk back to the front door as it starts to open.
Homeowner: What's up Doc?

Me: Hey, I didn't know you lived here. I see you at the church all the time.

Homeowner: You sure do. I'm Daryl. I sing tenor in the gospel choir.

Me: Oh, that's right you sing *Can't nobody do me like Jesus*. Man, you can bring it. Well the reason I'm here is, I'm looking for Shabazz. Have you seen him?

Daryl: Well…..no…....I USED to see him from time to time but, you know he stays in a lot of mess…...and I told him he needs to clean up his life before he comes back over here.

Me: (nodding) You don't mind if I look around for a second do you? Someone said they saw him walk in over here.

Daryl:(quickly) I don't think you need to be looking around right now since we are having a little get together.

Me: I won't take long. Besides, I don't want to get the police over here. They would want to embarrass people and ask a lot of questions.

Daryl: Yeah, you're right. Well try to make it quick.
Me: Thanks.

Walking toward the living room, I see two men and a woman looking like they are ignoring what's happening around them and staring at the TV. I glanced to see The Big Bang Theory was on. No Shabazz under the couch. Nothing around the dishes cabinet. My first thought was, why people have old dishes that no one ever eats on in a cabinet? Then I glanced at Daryl while I was moving around. His face looked nervous, he was standing near a window looking down. I continued to the bedroom to the right side of the house. I opened the door to a small bedroom with shoes and clothes all over the floor. Looking under the bed, I see boxes and more clothes. I go to the closet, more clothes and shoes. I walked into the other bedroom on the left there are six kids sitting on the bed. Just sitting. Facing the door.

Kids: Hey. (all in unison)

Me: Hey, ya'll. Is everybody having fun tonight?

Kids: Yes sir.

I started looking under the bed and, in the closet, and saw more of the same clothes and shoes. The only rooms left was a bathroom down the hall and the kitchen. I opened the back door and see Deva, still back there, ready to grab Shabazz.

Me: Did you see anything?

Deva: No. Nothing.

Me: I saw him in the living room on the couch when I walked up. It's only two bedrooms. He didn't have enough time to get up in the attic. Come on in. He's got to be in here.

 I started walking by the room with the kids in it. In the same spot as before.

Kids: Hey.Hey.

Me: Hey kids.

They looked like they were all on punishment. I decided to walk in further and saw the bed looking a little bumpy in the middle. I reach over and press the lump and one of the kids starts to giggle.

Me: Hey kids could you guys get off the bed for a second?

 With the kids scattered and my hand lifting the corner of the bed, I see the impression of a man's hand imprinted on the mattress. I pulled the mattress up further to see, Shabazz hand sliding back.

Me: Got him Deva! He's in here!
I grab Shabazz's arm and start pulling him out from between the mattress and the kids take off into the other room running.

Shabazz: Hey Doc! I wasn't running.
Me: (laughing) I know you always sleep like this.

Deva came up behind me and starts patting Shabazz down.
I pulled out my lucky handcuffs placing them on Shabazz, and we all started walking, out toward the front door. I looked over at Daryl, and he was looking away kind of like he was embarrassed about the situation. Walking back to the car, we passed several people looking.

Shabazz: How did you know I was over there?

Me: When you went past, Robinson Park some of my people saw you.

Shabazz: Man, those are some nosy people around there…….Can we stop and get something to eat on the way to the jail? You know the food won't ready yet, over at Daryl's.

Me: I'll ask Deva to pull through McDonald's on the way. You got McDonalds money?

Shabazz: Not right now, but I can pay you back when I get out of jail.

Me: I should give you my bank account number so you can make the deposit.

I never get paid back when I loan money to someone going to jail. I handed Deva money for a Quarter Pounder with cheese meal then dropped Deva and Shabazz off at the Escalade. I hung back and watched as Deva got cranked after a try or two. Soon, I was on my way back home to get some rest. Doing the bail bonding business, you have to sleep when you can.

I had scheduled some house showings for a new client of mine Ms. Karen Wagner for the next morning. She is a smart executive in the insurance business and very demanding. She knows exactly what area she wants to be in and how much she is going to pay. I lined up three houses for the day in West Burlington. Two of which, I picked out and one that she had requested. Ms. Wagner was a beautiful woman, tall, with a dark complexion, and very shapely. I could tell that her climb up the ladder was well deserved, by the way she precisely detailed what she wanted. When dealing with someone with this type of personality, you have to stay on point with your information and be prepared to take extra steps. She always gives you the feeling like you could be replaced with a quick google search. I met Ms. Wagner through a friend that knew her from college. She was moving to Burlington to be centrally located for her job. She was responsible for a large area.

When I got home, I notice the garage door is open. Amari is putting her bicycle up when she sees me.

Amari: Hey daddy!

Me: What's up Amari?

Amari: May I go over to the neighbor's house?

Me: Ok. Where's your mom?

Amari: She's in the house watching her shows.

Me: Be home in an hour.

My wife likes to watch old foreign films. Lucky for me, we have a few T.V.'s in the house. When I get in the house, I see dinner still on the stove and Charita sitting on the couch with her feet up and a movie from the 60's on T.V.

Subtitles flashing across the bottom of the screen.

Me: How was your day?

Charita: It was great but, one of those little second graders grabbed my butt and started giggling.

Me: What did you do?

Charita: I told him to stop it! These kids today are a handful, with a thousand questions. How about you?
Me: I've been busy today.

I gave her the rundown about my day and went downstairs and cut on the T.V. It just happened to be on the news. The anchor was talking about Burlington having several people going to the hospital with hallucinations from some drug consumption. I turned the channel to the sports channel to watch the Golden State and Washington Wizards game. I love watching the North Carolina Guards go at it. Soon, Amari came in and asked to watch T.V., so I moved to the bedroom.

Chapter 4

*I'm your Bondsman that's
who I am and I'm
ready to bail whoever
I can call me early
Morning or late afternoon.*

My phone never stops. I checked the caller
I.D. and answer on speaker.

Me: What's up Putt?

Putt: Hey Doc, what's going on with all the
PCP mess the news is talking about? I'm
almost scared to get me a sack.

Me: Some fool is out there selling Marijuana,
laced with PCP. It's been hurting people.
Putt: I hope they find him before I do. You
know I don't need any problems right now. I
finally got me a job paying more than minimum
wage.

Me: Have you heard anything?

Putt: I believe your boy Ajax might have
something to do with it. He's got a lot going on
right now. I hear he's got a little gang going
around robbing people and selling weed.

Me: Yeah. I heard something about that, but he's out of town.

Putt: He still comes back and forth. I heard he was at the poker game at Roger's place last week and one of the guys at the game ended up in the hospital.

Me: Who was it?

Putt: T Slim from Beaumont apartments.

Me: How's he doing?

Putt: He's still in the hospital I guess, I don't know, I heard Ajax went back to Johnson City the day after it happened.

Me: Thanks. You be careful and let me know if you see or hear anything else about Ajax.

Putt: You know I got you.

The hunt for Ajax is starting to seem a little more urgent now that people are getting hurt. He's also gaining a lot of resources with his gang affiliations.
The next day at the office Latina was searching for information on some of our skips, while at the same time, planning her son's birthday party.

Me: What's going on with the birthday party? (I am the godfather of Latina's youngest son) Any strippers going to pop out the cake?

Latina: Not this time. I'm the only woman he better be looking at for his 3rd birthday. (laughing) I was thinking about getting some Marvel superheroes to come by. You know some of them are kinda hot.

Me: I can't wait. You know, Deva, and I are going to Johnson City Saturday morning to try and get Ajax.

Latina: Well, good luck. We need to get him off the books, I called some of the bail skips that came in the mail the other day. J Rock's people said he's not coming in and he's acting crazy. They told him we would be coming for him.

I'm your Bondsman that's
who I am and I'm
ready to bail whoever
I can call me early
Morning or late afternoon.

Me: Hello?

Poochie: Hey baby, what are you up to this morning?

Me: Just hanging around the office. What's up with you?

Poochie: I was wondering if you could help me out? My cousin is acting like she is a prophet and thinking everybody is after her.

Me: Have you called the police?

Poochie: You know I'm not going to do that. What should I do?

Me: Will she go with you to the hospital? There's some PCP going around, and she might have gotten a hold of some. Who is she getting her weed from? Some of these guys aren't legit.

Poochie: I bet that T Slim is selling that mess. He came up here with some weed to sell. He's always trying to sell some fake drugs.

Me: T-Slim is in the hospital with the same symptoms. I thought?

Pooche: I'll check on it. Somebody gonna get killed with this mess going around. You know T slim and J Rock likes to go up to Elon and mess around with those rich kids. They smoke anything.

Me: I will see what I can find out but take her to the hospital and get her checked out.

Poochie: Ok. thanks baby.

Carter walked into the office.

Carter: Doc Reaves!

Me: What's up, CC?

Carter: Boy, June called me laughing his head off. He told me you choked on the last hole the other day I know that's not true.

Me: I didn't choke. I got a phone call in my backswing.

Carter: I knew it was something. You don't lose without some excuse.

Me: That's not an excuse. That's what happened. I pulled the putter back and when I started my stroke through, my phone started vibrating in my pocket.

Carter: Riiiiight….. Hey Ms. Latina, how are you doing today?

Latina: Hey Mr. Carter, I'm doing fine. How's Mrs. Carter doing?

Carter: She's good, out walking this morning.

Latina: Tell her I said hi!

Carter: I will baby. (in a Barry White tone).

Me: You know I'm after June now?

June walks around the corner and into the office.

June: What's up choke artist?

Me: You know you've made my list.

June: When did I ever get off it? (with a big grin)

*I'm your Bondsman that's
who I am and I'm
ready to bail whoever
I can call me early
Morning or late afternoon.*

Me: Reaves

Kat: Hey Doc. Can you come down to the jail? I believe somebody's trying to set me up. The police are here tearing the place up. I'm getting ready to get taken to jail now. (click)

They locked me up with
no place to go, they took
my clothes and stole
my doe. I'm in a cell on
A pay phone, call my
bondsman and get me
 home. (Get me home)

Me: Hey Deva can you go down to the jail? Kat said they came in on him and are taking him to the jail?

Deva: So he hasn't got a bond yet?

Me: Nope. Not yet, but it's Kat. You know he's going to have one.

Deva: Alright, I'll go down there.

We never go to the jail until after the bond is set. You never know when people will get a recognized bond or no bond at all, and then you'd have to wait for a judge to set it. Carter and June were talking about some golf tournament that Tiger Woods was going to play in and some of the new pros on tour right now.

Me: You guys going to be around for a while? I've got to meet with one of my clients and show her a house.

June: One of your clients, huh, like you have more than one. I don't see a whole lot of Real Estate going on around here.

The guys decided to head out and do a little practicing on their putting and chipping on the golf course.
It only took a few moments to look at the houses I had picked out for Ms. Wagner. She wasn't impressed. One was too big and the other in the wrong location; So, we continued to the house she had picked out, and it was love at first sight.

Ms. Wagner: This home has a lot of detail in it and only two miles from the interstate. What do you think?

Me: I like it. The bonus room is large, and the designs on the floor are great. I also like the design of the Master bedroom on the other side of the house.

Ms. Wagner: I want to put in an offer. I noticed it has been on the market for a little while, so maybe they will take a lot less. They can't afford to let it sit. What do you think about two hundred and sixty thousand?

Me: That sounds good to me. I'll get it written up and start the negotiations.

I called Latina and told her about the offer and all the particulars so she could get started writing it up. I headed over to check on Kat.

Chapter 5

Kat is a frequent client of mine because of his connections to the streets. He calls for his associates as well as himself. Whenever the police arrest him, it looks like they are targeting him because of his nice cars, and designer clothes that make him look like he came out of GQ magazine. He's also always posting pictures of him and some hot girls.

Most days, he goes shopping and riding around like he just hit the lottery.

When I got to the jail, the magistrate had a couple of people in line. Deva was there with some of the new younger bondsmen waiting on their turn at the window. The only way a bail bondsman can come to the jail is if they have some business there, and soliciting is strictly prohibited. The young guys were talking with some potential clients. New bondsmen will get anybody out of jail for half the price, trying to build up clients and make some fast money. I've seen this backfire more than a few times because of mismanagement of the money, not being able to find the skips or pay the forfeitures. All the money paid for not catching bail skips goes into the school system.

Deva walks over.

Deva: Look at that kid over there wearing his company t-shirt, advertising he's with *Acme Bail Bonds*. They do those three percent bonds.

Which is a bait and switch. They get you to call them for a 3 percent bond, then they set you up on payments you can't make for fifteen percent. When you miss one payment, they come and lock you back up, and walk away without a chance to get your money back.

Deva: I told that guy not to wear that shirt down here anymore.

With Deva's size, I would think the kid wouldn't want to mess with him like that, but these young kids don't listen to anybody. It comes from taking paddling out of schools, in my opinion.
Deva Headed straight for him.

Deva: Hey man, I thought I told you that the shirt was advertising and you couldn't wear it down here?

Acme kid: I called the State. They said it was fine.

Soon a female bail agent came in with a briefcase with *Ebony Bail Bonds* on it. "We do financing three percent down, payment plans and 24/7 service give me a call!!" with her phone number on the side. Deva and the kid looked around at the same time the agent set her briefcase down and walked back out to her car.

Deva: (Looked at the kid) Do you see what you started?

Acme Kid: She can't do that why don't you say something to her?

Deva: She knows better. She is doing that to send a message to you.

The magistrate asked who was there for Mr. Williams. That was Kat's government name Deva stepped up to the window, and the magistrate started explaining.

Magistrate: Mr. Williams is charged with possession of a controlled substance and materials to sell and deliver marijuana. His bond is set at twenty thousand dollars. The officers wanted a higher bond on him because of his criminal history and the information they had gotten that, he was a major supplier, but they only found a small amount of weed and some scales.
The officers came out of the jail area.

Officer: Doc, are you getting Kat out? I know he's selling drugs. I can't get him like I want to but I know he's doing it and I'm going to stay on his tail until he quits or goes away for a long time.

Me: You know he tells me you guys are picking on him all the time.

Officer: That's almost comical, I know you don't believe that.

Me: I try to stay neutral.

Deva started writing the bond, and I waited to talk to Kat about the PCP problem. After about an hour of processing, Kat walked out of jail dressed in a dark blue Duke University sweat suit and was ready to get out of there. After Deva finished getting his information, that had changed since the last time we got him out of jail. I gave Kat a ride home so that we could talk in private.

Kat: Somebody had to send them over there. I just re-upped yesterday. If they had come over there then, I wouldn't have been able to make a bond with a million dollars. Man, that was close. They are about to make me hang this mess up. You should see the way they tore my house apart. Just tearing up stuff to mess with me. If they knew what they were doing, somebody would have found some real evidence in the house. The dogs couldn't get high enough to smell my money in the wall over my bed. I keep it behind my sex mirror in a fire safe, so it doesn't put out a strong odor. When we get to the house, I got your money for the bond.

Me: I need a little help on something. What do you know about that PCP going around?

Kat: Yeah, you know I'd heard about that mess. It has got everybody a little shook on the streets. I tell you this Doc, you know me. I wouldn't mess with something like that. I cook my stuff up myself. Some of those rich kids like to mess with their product like that. It's mixed with embalming fluid. You might want to go by a funeral home or something. I would talk to some of those kids over in Beaumont apartments. That's where T Slim stays. He's always doing some crazy stuff. I hope they find out who's doing it, they're hurting business.

We pulled into Kat's driveway, his cars were still there unlocked with papers laying all over the seats. The door to his house was wide open. The officers had busted the door open with a battering ram and threw a flash bomb in that had the house smelling like smoke. When we walked in you would have thought he, was robbed by someone with a vendetta against him. Clothes tossed everywhere, cabinets open, the freezer food on the kitchen table. Chairs and tables turned over, sofa cushions thrown to the floor, everything pulled away from the walls. I stayed in the living room and kitchen area while he went to the bedroom, and he came out counting twenties. I grabbed my receipt book and wrote him out a receipt for the money and headed out.

I'm your Bondsman that's
who I am and I'm
ready to bail whoever
I can call me early
Morning or late afternoon.

Me: Reaves

Poochie: Doc. I just saw T Slim and J Rock, that skip you were looking for, over in Beaumont Apartments. He was going in an apartment in the middle of the circle.

Me: Great. What's J Rock wearing?

Poochie: You know he's in that gang. He's always got on some green crap and some boots on with a Seattle Seahawks hat on that big head. I can't stand him. He's always stealing from somebody and acting like he's entitled or something. Watch him Doc. He's crazy.

Me: I'm going to head that way. Keep an eye on him. I'll text you when I get close.

Poochie: Cool. I had to walk off so I could call. These are some nosey folks around here, they all up in your business.

They locked me up with
no place to go, they took
my clothes and stole
my doe. I'm in a cell on
A pay phone, call my
bondsman and get me
 home. (Get me home)

Deva: What's up?

Me: Are you somewhere close?

Deva: I'm at the coffee shop chilling. What's up?

Me: J Rock is in Beaumont Apartments right now.

Deva: I'm on the way, you want to meet at Tommy's mini-mart?

Me: That's good with me, see you soon.

I met Deva at Tommy's mini-mart, about a quarter mile from Beaumont apartments and jumped in his gold Escalade. We pulled in and parked near the front of the apartments. I pulled out my small binoculars and started scanning for J Rock. While sitting there, a small kid, about three years old walked up to my side of the truck like he was doing an inventory of what we were doing. After a little while, I saw what looked like J Rock coming out of an apartment with two other guys and a bottle in his hand that looked like a forty.
Me: That's him Deva.

Deva hit the switch on the Truck. No Ignition. He hit it again and no fire. I looked at Deva.

Deva: Man. I just got this thing out of the shop!

Deva got out of the truck. He walked around to open the hood and the little fella came around looking at Deva while he tapped the battery and engine a few times. Deva climbed back in and hit the switch, it cranked. We slowly backed out and maintained a slow, steady speed, as J Rock was walking toward a silver Mustang parked in the parking lot. Deva pulls close, and I jumped out and ran up behind J Rock pulling my Taser.

The silver Mustang cranked up, and I saw Ajax. He hit the gas and drove around Deva spinning tires.

Me: Deva! Ajax is in the Mustang!

Deva had gotten out of the car and could only look as he was flying down and out of the apartments. We focused on what we came for. Deva was watching the other guys with J Rock, so they didn't try to jump me from behind. J Rock turned around and threw his 40-ounce bottle, it hit me in the shoulder, and he took off running. I fired the Taser catching him in the butt. His legs locked up, and he fell flat on his face as if someone had pushed over a mannequin. Then he started making the same noise that I had heard from Deva one time before. When I accidentally shot him with the Taser. J Rock tried to shake off the effects of the Taser, reaching for the electric cord and screaming in pain. I gave him another 15 second ride of juice.

Me: Roll over, and I'll cut it off.

J Rock: Urg Urg Urg

The power from that second jolt was starting to take the fight out of him. I put my knee in his back and got one cuff on. When he pulled his hands apart, Deva came over and moved me over with his weight landing on top of him, grabbing his un-cuffed hand. J Rock let out a yell while Deva locked the cuffs on and picked him up. I curled up the electric cord from the Taser, grabbed J Rock's arm, and threw them both in the truck. Deva jumped behind the wheel and grabbed J Rock's seat belt and snapped it in. I climbed in the back seat, and we backed out into the circle to drive out of the apartments. The same little kid was on my side of the car in the parking lot on the way out, acting like he was shooting a gun with his fingers as we went by.

Me: J Rock. what were you thinking about? I could have gotten hurt with you throwing that bottle like that.

J Rock: Doc. I can't go to jail man. I just started getting my life together.

Me: Why didn't you go to court? They might have worked with you and put you on probation or something.

J Rock: The police are trying to tie me to that PCP mess because I was in the area when a funeral home got broken into last year. They locked me up, and I wasn't doing nothing!

Me: Well you did have burglary tools in your property bag, when we bailed you out.

J Rock: See. If you say that, what do you think the judge is going to say? Man, I knew I shouldn't have been messing with that gang mess. They make you go out and do some of the craziest things. First carjacking's and then breaking into buildings. You know I only steal to eat and get high. Besides, won't nobody give me a job with my record.

Me: That green you are wearing is Ajax gang colors isn't it? What was he doing over there? You know I've been looking for him?

J Rock: Man, you know the green is to clean. Ajax cleans everything. At least that's what he tells everybody. Doc. I'll talk to you because I know you won't say nothing. That Ajax is doing some crazy stuff out here man. He even got my man T Slim messed up. I thought he was dead for real. The drugs he used that sent him to the hospital came from Ajax. He had come over there complaining that he wasn't getting all his money or something. I'm kinda glad you showed up. I was about to have to deal with him myself.

Me: Where is Ajax staying nowadays?

J Rock: I could use a little something to eat Doc, when we go by a restaurant.

Me: I got you. Where do you want to stop?

J Rock: I'd like a steak since I'm going to be there awhile. Won't nobody get me out with that fail to appear on my record will they?

Me: You can have McDonalds or Burger King. Take your pick. Maybe one of those new companies, will get you back out.

J Rock: Mickie Ds all day! Ajax stays in Johnson City somewhere. I've never been over there. Man, these guys treat him like he's John Jones. They know what he's doing but won't stop working for him. It's like a cult or something.

Me: That is crazy. I don't have a lot of time left. He missed court a while ago and my time is running out.

J Rock: If you let me go, I'll let you know when he shows up again.

Me: That's not going to happen.

J Rock: Get me two-quarter pounders. No cheese. I got to stay away from that dairy. Those guys in the jail get pissed off about all the gas. Supersize me the fries and an orange soda with an apple pie.

Me: That all?

J Rock: Also, get me a happy meal with a handcuff key in it.

Me: Sure thing.

When we got to the sally port of the jail, there were cars everywhere. Deva parked on the outside of the sally port and we walked in. Every law enforcement group was represented. Highway Patrol, SBI, Burlington Police, Graham Police and surrounding counties. We walked up with J Rock and got in line. The Sheriff had a roundup going on. They were calling it, operation PCP. One of the detectives recognized J Rock and said, "Thanks Doc, he was on our list for today". Several guys arrested were asking Deva and me to get them out and make some calls for them. The officers weren't letting anyone make any phone calls so they could keep the element of surprise.

Chapter 6

The next morning was Friday and tee time was at 10:10am. June was on the putting green warming up when I got there. When I walked up, he never looked up. He just kept working on his putting. I don't know if it was the anticipation or the lack of practice, but we played terrible the whole way around the course. On the last hole, I had a chance to beat June a couple of bets for the day with a 10 ft. putt. I stroked the putt and it hit the hole dead center.

June: That wasn't nothing to brag about right there, we were horrible. I feel like I beat myself.

Me: I don't like to play bad, but anytime I beat you I've had a great day. We may go to the movies tonight thanks to you. (chuckling to myself)

June: You can laugh all you want. This ain't over.

I checked my email and saw that Ms. Wagner had gotten the contract on the house she wanted, so I gave her a call.

Ms. Wagner: Hello?

Me: Ms. Wagner, we have a contract on your house on Jefferson Ln.

Ms. Wagner: Whoo Hoo!! That's good news! I've been looking at some furniture that would go well with it. So, what do we do now?

Me: I'm going to get Latina to email you a copy of the contract to take to the bank, and you can start the loan process. I will get in touch with your attorney and give him all the information.

Ms. Wagner: Thanks a lot. This has been kind of easy. Good job.

Saturday morning, Deva and I drove up to Johnson City in a rental car so that we could get close without being spotted. We called Detective Gasparello on the way to Johnson City. He told us that we could meet at the station and he would give me the key to the apartment, close to Ajax's hangout. Detective Gasparello was Italian with olive skin, a raspy voice about 5'9", dark hair and a calm demeanor.

Gasparello: How's it going? I'm glad you could make it up. We've wanted to talk with him about a murder that took place, but we couldn't get our hands on him. He was locked up on some other charge when it happened so we know he couldn't have done the crime, but someone in his circle probably did. If you guys don't mind, could you stop him by the Bristol police department so the homicide detectives could have a little chat with him before you take him back to North Carolina?

Me: Not a problem. We'll make sure they can question him.

Gasparello read off the address and gave me a key to the apartment. The drive was only about eight minutes from the station and the time was around 1:00 pm. The apartment is on the first floor. There were two bedrooms with a living room area and the kitchen stocked with drinks and food. The furniture looks vintage, to be kind. The view of the apartment Ajax was hanging out at was perfect. It's a second-floor apartment about mid-way through the complex on the left of the stairs. Ajax couldn't come in or out without us seeing him. Deva drew first watch on the apartment while I stretched out on the couch and cut the TV on to watch Carolina play Georgia Tech in basketball. Cars kept coming in and out with someone going into the apartment and then reappearing, leaving the apartment. At times, there would be people coming out to stand on the walkway and look around. Two hours passed when Deva said there was a skinny guy with a gray beard coming to our door.

BANG. BANG.BANG. Deva pulled open the door.

Deva: Can I help you?

Gray Beard: What the hell are y'all doing in my momma's apartment?!

Me: What do you mean? The detective gave us this apartment for the day.

Graybeard: I already called the police, and you are going to jail.

Me: Hey, look. Can we go around to the side of the building? I'll call detective Gasparello.

A police car was pulling into the parking lot behind him as we were talking, with the lights going. Deva grabbed the bags and started walking towards our car. Graybeard and I started walking around the side of the building out of sight of Ajax's apartment. The officer put his hand on his firearm as he was walking over to us. He's slim, about 6'1", about 30 yrs. old, and looking intense.

Graybeard: OVER HERE!! (while waving his hands and pointing at me).

Officer: Let me see those hands!
Me: Officer. I know this looks bad, but if you could call Detective Gasparello he can explain what's going on. I'm Doc Reaves. I'm a bail bondsman from North Carolina. We have a good reason for being here. (I raise my hands up about shoulder width)

Graybeard: I want them locked up!! That's what yawl do to me. There's another one, over there by that car.

The officer waved for Deva to come over, drawing his weapon. Deva, by his size alone is intimidating.

Officer: I'll call Gasparello and see what's going on. You guys stay against that wall with your hands on your heads.

A few minutes later the officer started chuckling and returned over to Me and Deva.

Officer: You guys are free to leave. Gasparello said he didn't realize the landlord had rented out this apartment. He is going to call the hotel you were at last time, and get you guys a good rate on a room. He said he's sorry about the confusion.

Me: Thanks a lot.

Graybeard: That's some bull!! What if they stole something? You wouldn't let me go like that. I'm going to sue somebody.

I apologized to Graybeard and his mom, and we headed to the hotel. Hopefully Ajax wasn't inside the apartment when this all went down because he would have recognized us and left. On the way to the hotel, we stopped for Deva to get something to eat at *Texas Road House*. Deva ordered enough for three men and told the server exactly how he wanted each entrée prepared. About 2 hours later, Deva and I checked into the hotel.
Around 9:00 pm we went back over to the apartment and found a parking spot adjacent to the apartment and staked it out for three hours. The apartment was on fire with activity.

Gray beard came out of his momma's apartment walking over to Ajax apartment. He went in. Stayed about two minutes and walked out. At around 12:00 am. we went back to the hotel and got some sleep.

The next morning after breakfast we went back over and sat. Ajax never came in or out. I leaned over to Deva:

Me: We need to go to the apartment and make sure Ajax isn't in there watching Netflix.

I decided to drive to the front of the apartment complex. Deva and I climbed the steps. I had my 40. Glock on my ankle and Deva had a small 380. in his pocket. I knocked on the door, and a young guy came to the door. He looked sleepy, with dreads, wearing pajama bottoms and barefoot. The apartment had the smell of weed, with a worn-out couch and mixed match chairs. A large screen TV was hooked up to a PlayStation and two guys were in the middle of a game of football. Another guy was watching as if he had next.

Me: I'm Shed. Ajax uncle. I'm supposed to be meeting him here. (As we walked in) Have you seen him? I'm only going to be here for a minute.

Dread head: I haven't seen him today, but I can call him if you have a phone?

I pulled my flip phone out and gave it to Dreads, not thinking about the words bail life on the front cover, but he never noticed it and started dialing. The phone went immediately to voicemail like it was declined or turned off. Dreads handed the phone back to me. I had gone to school with Ajax Uncle Shed, so I tried to imitate his voice, and leave a message on his voicemail.

Me: Hey Ajax this is your Uncle Shed. I'm not going to be here, all day. (*click* I hung up).

A guy came from the back bedroom looking at Deva holding a .38 snub nose pistol.

The Guy from backroom: Do you want to buy a .38? I'm selling it for fifty dollars.

Deva: Nah, man. I don't need a gun bro.

The guys all seemed like they waited on Ajax to give them their orders, so they gave us respect also.

Me: I'm going to ride around and see what we can get into around here. We'll be back later.

Deva and I walked out and went back to the car. I cranked up and rode around behind the apartments. The road led to a dead end with a view over a cliff to a lake that was absolutely beautiful, with a lot of trees and some railing to keep people from running off the edge. We pulled over and talked about my performance.

Deva: Man, Doc you went into a character worthy of an academy award.

Me: I felt like I embraced my role.

Soon, we were driving back toward the hotel. From a distance I saw a silver mustang heading toward us. Ajax was driving right by us heading toward the apartment. I kept watching him in my rearview until he turned to go toward the apartment building. I turned into a gas station and started driving toward the apartment.
When I turned the corner to the apartment, Ajax was still sitting in the car. His passenger, a young white lady, had gone up to the hangout spot. I pulled right up to Ajax Mustang's bumper. Deva and I jumped out with guns pointing directly at Ajax. He froze staring at the barrels. The apartment door flew open, and the guys started to come down the

steps. I swung around with my Glock, pointing right at Dreads.

Me: Bail bondsman. Don't come down those steps.

Everybody on the walkway stopped. Looking at Ajax for some instructions.

Me: Go ahead and get him Deva. I'll watch them.

Deva walked over and pulled Ajax out of the car at gunpoint. He was surprised we had found him in Johnson City. Deva hooked the cuffs on, walked him over to the car and sat him down in the front seat. Deva switched out the handcuffs for the leg irons and short chains.

Young Lady: Can I bring him his money?

Me: You come down. Nobody else.

She handed him a wad of cash and kissed him on the lips.

Ajax: Go by the apartment and get the rest and come to

Burlington and get me out of jail. How much is my bond going to be?

Me: It should be about ten thousand dollars if you pay the whole thing, but if you get a bail bondsman it would be a thousand dollars.
 I shut the door and jumped in. Deva got in the back, and we took off.
ring. ring.ring

Gasparello: Hello?

Me: We just picked up Ajax.

Gasparello: Could you stop by Bristol and let some of the detectives talk with him?

Me: No problem. We should be there in about 20 minutes.

Gasparello: I will give them your number so you can hook up. Great job fellas! We appreciate you guys taking that trash out of here.

Me: Thanks for your help Detective.

We pulled up in Bristol which was right off of the Highway. Two officers were waiting. A woman and a man in plain clothes. I opened the door. The officers came over with a file in their hands with pictures and information about a young girl that had been hanging around with his crew and ended up dead in the woods. Ajax just looked at the officers.

Detectives: I know you were in jail when this happened, but we need to get some closure for this family.

Ajax: I don't know what the hell you guys are talking about.

Detectives: That's all you got to say? This girl was murdered with a .38 revolver and you don't give a darn. That's about as sorry as it gets. Take that piece of crap back to North Carolina.

There wasn't a lot of talk from Alex on the way back to Graham. Deva and I were talking about the ball game coming on next week between Carolina and North Carolina State when...

I'm your Bondsman that's
who I am and I'm
ready to bail whoever
I can call me early
Morning or late afternoon.

Me: Reaves.

Sheriff: Doc, this is the Sheriff. My detectives tell me that an Alex Chandler is the one putting this PCP out on the street. He goes by Ajax now. You bailed him out last year sometime, and he skipped court. What kind of information have you got on him? This thing is getting serious. Someone just died from running out in front of a car on this mess.

Me: Wow. Somebody died. That's a shame. Well I've got some great info Sheriff. Do you want to talk to him now? He's right beside me. Me and Deva just picked him up.

Sheriff: Hot Damn!! You know I love you guys!! Tell that big one I'm going to take you guys out to lunch. Put me on speaker, Doc.

I put my phone on speaker so that Ajax could hear the sheriff.

Sheriff: Son, I want you to know you are going to the chair, if I get my way about it. You have caused this county more grief than you know and I'm going to do everything in my power to make you pay for it dearly.

There was a long pause. Then.....

Ajax: I don't know what you are talking about I didn't have nothing to do with no PCP.

Sheriff: Well that's not what all the evidence I've got is saying, and witnesses that will put you dead and I mean to say D E A D in it. Thanks, Doc. How far out are you guys?

Me: I'm about an hour and a half away. We are coming from Johnson City.

Sheriff: I will see you when you get here, and lunch is on me.

The Sheriff hung up, and I saw Ajax thinking hard.

Ajax: Man, this is crazy. I know I've done some bad stuff, but I swear on my momma's grave I didn't know about the PCP, until that crazy tail T Slim went to the hospital. I was on my way back to Johnson City when crazy J Rock called me talking about him and T Slim had made a lick at Elon on those rich kids, and something had gone wrong. He said they had started hanging out with the kids and getting high with them. One day they went over there, and the kids had a big bag of weed sitting on a table. They all left to go to a party, so they stole the dope. They had been putting that mess out on the street for days and T Slim, being the dumb butt, he is, decided to get high on his own supply. That's what put him in the hospital. I guarantee that J Rock and T Slim's down there running their mouths trying to get this mess off of them. I know they can't pin this mess on me, can they?

Me: I don't know. It depends on who the Sheriff believes.

Ajax started thinking hard trying to get his story straight for the Sheriff. Me and Deva did what we always do.

Deva: Hey, Doc. Why is it when a female sees a woman that isn't all that attractive, they compliment something about her, but when they look at a ten, they find something negative to say?

Me: Competition. They don't want you looking at the ten with admiration, without seeing their flaws. I hadn't noticed it, but I will start paying attention to it now.

Deva: We haven't been to a club in a long time together. You remember when we used to go to the club every Friday night after our rounds? I miss those days.

We talked all the way back to the sally port. I pushed the button on the speaker.

Me: This is Reaves. I'm bringing one in.

Speaker operator: What's up Doc? The Sheriff is waiting on you. I'll tell him you're here. Come on in the gate. Go to intake bay number two.

The gate opened, and we drove up, as bay #2 was opening. I drove all the way to the end of the bay. Two plain clothes detectives came out to meet us as we were getting out of the car.

Detective: We'll take him from here Doc. I got your file numbers for your surrenders, so we'll serve them for you.

Ajax: I had nothing to do with that PCP mess.
Detective: Don't worry. You'll get to tell your side after we read you your rights.

Deva and I got back in the car and started toward Deva's apartment. I know Ajax was throwing everybody under the bus. He was shaken by the Sheriff telling him he was getting the death penalty.
Over the next week the Sheriff had T Slim and half of the Ajax gang locked up. After searching T Slim's apartment, they found

some weed with embalming fluid in it. The containers stolen from the funeral home were still in the closet. Ajax must have been convincing while talking with the detectives he made bond at 50,000.00 with Acme bail bonds at 3 percent, which is cheap considering the crimes he's charged with. My theory is his amnesia cleared up about the murder in Bristol, the whereabouts of a particular .38 snub nose revolver, and the person holding the gun when it was used in the murder.
 Gasparello called to thank me again. Sunday was my day to usher at church, and the preacher was talking about the Sheriff making an arrest on the PCP case and the upcoming funeral for the young man that had gotten hit with the car while on PCP. He needed some ushers for Monday around 1:00pm. I looked at the other usher on the door opposite of me thinking "Any day but Monday or Friday"

I'm your Bondsman that's
who I am and I'm
ready to bail whoever
I can call me early
Morning or late afternoon.
I slipped out the door I was watching.

Me: Reaves.

Jason White: I need your help. I put my house up for bond on a young lady, and now she won't go to court. Can you help?

www.ingramcontent.com/pod-product-compliance
Lightning Source LLC
Chambersburg PA
CBHW020642130626
46552CB00003B/1366